THE WHISPERERS

A CHILDREN'S MYSTERY ADVENTURE

BRENDA LARKIN

HALLABALOO PUBLISHING

To Cleo and James
with love

CONTENTS

Map of THE OLD LAND

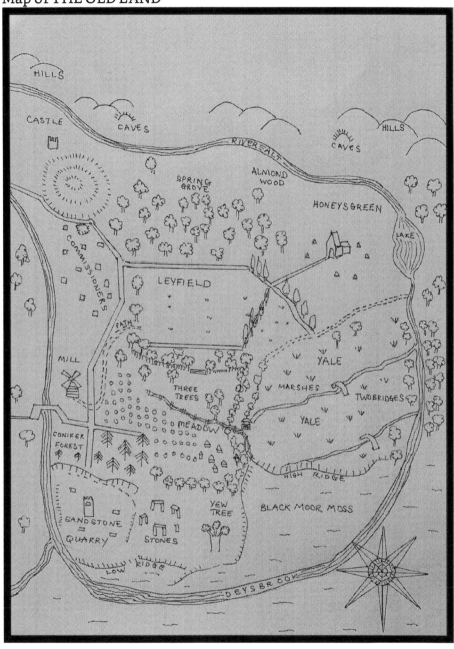

1 THE MILL

When the dark will call
And lure through the age's gate
The sun will shine with moon over fields
Set the path to where it leads.

Oddly, my mum won the lottery. She went into the co-op in the village one night, 'on a whim,' she said, and jotted down the first six odd numbers that popped into her head. The next day, Mum, my little sister, Seren and me, Tyus, woke up with half a million pounds.

After the shock and excitement, Mum said it wasn't enough to retire on or squander on fripperies. We would be allowed one sensible thing each. I chose a bike and Seren chose a doll that looks and sounds like a baby. Mum had decided she was going to fulfill her life's dream and open a dance school.

Ugh! Not for me, I'll say that quickly. I'm ten and not into dancing but Seren, who is eight, seemed excited by it. Mum was going to look for an old house that she could turn in to a dance studio and our family could live upstairs.

So we bought the Old Mill House, which had been empty for years and moved in. The Mill House stood at the edge of the village, away from other properties, hidden by a huge sandstone wall. It was a large, rambling building with round windows and a long, narrow garden, overgrown with brambles and untidy privets.

Strangely, it had never come up for sale but the day Mum received her winning cheque from the solicitor in his office, he told her that it had suddenly become available. Immediately, Mum made an offer and it was accepted. It was going to take months of work to make it how she wanted but it was just right. The enormous ground floor could be turned into a studio. There was an attic where the caretaker had lived that would be comfortable for us to live in while the renovations were done. Seren and I would have our own bedroom but as Seren sometimes sleepwalks, Mum and I are often 'on alert.' If she ever 'woke up' in the night, Mum and I would follow her around the house and keep her safe until she went back to bed.

Seren has been sleepwalking since she was four, and the doctors say she will grow out of it one day. Thankfully, she doesn't sleepwalk often now but we still listen out for her at night. It was the trauma, said one doctor, the shock she had when she was little. She had had an enormous shock.

Seren was out with our Dad and he 'disappeared'.

He had fallen down a well or been eaten by the ground was all she could say. She wasn't making sense. There was no well or sinkhole just grass. She was found standing alone in the park, crying. The police brought her home and we've never seen Dad since. They searched for him for a bit but it was like he had vanished into thin air.

Mum couldn't believe it. Dad would never leave us she was sure. For the last four years she has been looking for him. She checked with his friends, even hired private detectives to try to find him but nothing, no sign of him anywhere. She was about to give up the search when she won the lottery prize. *This is a turning point for us* she said. Maybe starting a new life would help Seren. Oddly, winning the lottery was a chance to look to the future rather than the past. When we settled into our new house, she would begin the hunt for Dad again.

I can remember my Dad clearly. He was big and jolly and kind. People say Seren and I both look like him- tall and golden haired. We come from Viking stock he would claim. He played football with me, sat me on his shoulders, told silly jokes and read bedtime stories. He would cook pasta and we would all dance in the kitchen. I would climb on Dad's shoulders and Mum would dance with Seren in her arms. We'd jiggle and giggle to the music. Mum would say we all needed to join her imaginary dance school for proper lessons and Dad would laugh. He would be in his imaginary garage restoring vintage cars.

His big hobby was metal. He would go metal detecting with special equipment searching for treasure. He never found anything valuable though, just bottle tops, nails and rusty tools. Mum was sure he had enough scrap metal to make a car if he wanted.

My favourite activity now is using my dad's old metal detector. I cycle out to the parkland where he disappeared and take out the metal detector. I let it hover over the ground listening for the noises in the earphones that tell me if there is old metal beneath the soil. Maybe Dad found gold coins or treasure here and he bought a vintage car and is travelling round the world. Inside I know this is not true. The only treasure I've found were the usual bottle tops.

Where did you go, Dad?

Here we are, living in the Old Mill House. Most of the work has been done. It has been plastered and painted. Plumbers, electricians and builders have transformed the crumbling mill into a smart dance studio and a comfortable home for us. Finally, our lives were settling down at last.

It was Friday night when it happened. Mum's dream was coming true. She was working on posters and her website for the dance studio. She was excited, as the studio was almost ready for the grand opening. Seren was over-excited as she had been allowed to dance on the new dance floor and she had loved it. Its shiny wood was springy like a dull trampoline and gave you the idea you could jump higher or leap further than you have ever imagined. I had a feeling Seren might find it difficult to go to sleep at bedtime but I was wrong, she fell asleep quickly.

'Ah, she's exhausted, poor lamb.' Mum said yawning as she popped in to say good night. 'Let's all get a good night's sleep.'

We said goodnight and I think I slept a bit because I had a dream about being at school and being locked in one of the classrooms.

The dream woke me up so I went to check on Seren. My sister was gone.

I knew it. I bet she's sleepwalking. I grabbed my hoodie and put it on over my pyjamas, slipped on my trainers and ran out of the door. I didn't call Mum as I thought Seren couldn't have gone far. I scampered downstairs. The studio door was opened. She must be in there dancing again. I rushed in but there was no one there just my dark reflection on all four walls from the ceiling to floor mirrors. I stared at each wall and my face stared back at me - wide eyed, washed out and worried.

I ran into the hall - the front door was locked. Right, she didn't get out. She must be inside somewhere, I thought. I tried the lounge, the kitchen – nothing, but there was a sliver of light coming from the small larder room. I tiptoed over and pulled back the door. No Seren.

The light was coming from a small trap door on the floor that I'd never seen before. Surely she hadn't squeezed down there. I opened the door and the light went out.

I grabbed a torch from the larder shelf and shone the beam down the trap door. There was a short ladder leading down to a room under the house. Seren's new doll lay at the bottom of the ladder. So, she did come this way.

I didn't know we had a cellar, I thought as I clambered down the ladder. I didn't want to shout incase I frightened Seren but if she had gone down there she was alone and would be upset and distressed, I had to follow. I stretched up and placed the doll back up in the larder room.

It was dark and I'm no hero but if my little sister was in trouble. I have to help. She must be just along this passageway…

2 THE LEY FIELD

A single watcher waits
As o'er the land he walks and tends
Challengers and holds the crown
To show the travellers through time.

The passageway was narrow. The brick walls were wet and crumbling, glistening in the torchlight. I shone the torch straight ahead but could not see the end. I started to think I should go and fetch Mum but thinking about Seren made me press on. Is this some huge cellar under the house? If our house was originally an old mill, maybe there would have been a workshop here or a room for storing grain. Mum hadn't mentioned it.

I was getting worried. The passageway was sloping lower. Suddenly, I saw a light flickering ahead.

'Seren?' I whispered. I picked up my pace and shone my torch towards the light and there was a face - Seren!

I took hold of her shoulders gently to see if she was sleepwalking but she was perfectly awake. I breathed a sigh. She laughed.

'Tyus, you should see this!'

Taking me by the hand she led me from the tunnel.

'What are you doing here? You should be in bed.' I hissed.

'I know but I went to get a glass of water and I saw a door open with lots of twinkly lights so I followed them. Look!' Her face glowed with amusement.

'It was complete darkness when I was there. What are you talking about?'

I was confused even more with what I saw before me: a field - a large open field, green grass, no fences or gates. And it was daytime. It was bright and sunny. The colours were vivid after being in the dark passageway. I rubbed my eyes. Sheep in the distance, cows grazing. It looked like a glorious sunny afternoon in the countryside.

'What is this?' I gasped.

Seren was still chuckling. 'Isn't it great? It's like our own special farm under our house.'

She ran about and started doing cartwheels on the grass.

'Yes,' I said, 'and that's not normal. Let's get out of here and tell Mum.'

I took her by the hand and bundled her back into the direction of the tunnel as best I could.

'Don't go Master!' a shrill voice said. 'Please, sit thee here. Take some refreshment.'

I froze. I squeezed Seren's hand tightly. I needed to know I wasn't dreaming myself.

'Ouch! That hurts, Ty!' she cried.

Turning slowly, setting my face in a scowl to appear fierce, I glared at the owner of the voice.

A man, small, slight with a round smiling face; two large pools for eyes and wearing a dress - well, a tunic I think you call it, tied with a rough, ropey belt. It was knee length and his bare, skinny legs were criss-crossed with ribbon, which tied on to his pointy shoes.

'Would Master take some milk, fresh this morning?' he continued unfazed by my stern features.

He offered me an earthenware cup of cold white milk.

'We have been waiting many years for thee. I be honoured to be the first to greet thee. Welcome to the Ley Field.'

My scowl had not scared him like I intended and although he seemed polite I was not having anything to do with him or his milk. I've been warned about 'stranger danger' many times.

'No thank you,' I said firmly, mustering the strongest voice I could. 'We're leaving.'

Pulling Seren's arm, I forced her back towards the tunnel.

'Let's go quickly!'

Seren resisted.

'No, I want to explore this place, Ty. I'll have the milk if my brother doesn't want it.'

She reached out to take the cup but I stopped her. She frowned at me angrily.

'It's the middle of the night, Seren; you should be in bed. I should be in bed – and not in this place.' My eyes scanned the field and gasped.

It was beautiful. The bluest, cloudless sky, soft green grass, yellow buttercups sprinkled across the field, tranquil cows and the weirdo! We're going.

The little man danced about jerkily, spilling the milk.

'Master Ty, we have need of thee - only thou can help us. Only thou know how to free the Whisperers.'

'How do you know my name? What is this place? What are you talking about? Who are the whisperers?'

I was getting louder and more worried. I could see he was becoming more agitated as he skipped in circles.

'Goldenhair said ye would come one day to the Ley Field, Master Ty - this be where thou are and I was to give thee this.'

He took a small, rusty bottle top from his tunic and placed it on his outstretched palm. Immediately, I shivered then a flush rushed to my cheeks. I picked up the bottle top from his parchment like hand and examined it. I knew at once it was one of Dad's metal detecting finds.

'Take me to him!'

3 THE MEADOW

Nourish and nature
Fire and warmth
Strength and loyalty
Guide through the morn.

'**H**urray, does that mean we can stay?' Seren jumped up and down but then seeing my serious face, she stopped.

'What is it, Ty?'

I lowered my voice.

'I don't know what's happening here but you should go back home while I find out.'

'If you're staying, I'm staying!' Seren cried.

'Look!' I showed her the metal disc. 'This is exactly like the bottle tops Dad used to bring home after he went metal detecting.'

I glanced over my shoulder to see the little man hopping about from one leg to another.

'What is he doing with it? I don't know what this place is but I think Dad is here somewhere and I have to find him.'

Seren flipped the bottle top over between her finger and thumb. She stared at it thoughtfully.

'No, *we* have to find him. I want to stay.'

'Master and mistress, may I present myself to you. I am Odo of the Ley Field. I look after the animals that graze here.' Odo gave a bow.

'Amazing, you own all this?' smiled Seren.

Odo chuckled. 'No, this is common land. The cattle and such belong, like everything else, to the Commissioners. I am merely a herdsman. I watch, I wait, I tend. That is why I am here – to wait for ye.'

'Who are the Commissioners? Why do they want you to wait for us? And who gave you this bottle top?'

'Master, be careful.' Odo suddenly stood still. ' Goldenhair asked me to wait, not the Commissioners. If they knew ye had arrived they would be here to arrest thee and the young Mistress. Goldenhair said once ye came to live in the Old Mill House, ye would find us.'

'How did you know about our house?' cried Seren.

Odo nodded. 'It is true.'

'So Goldenhair gave you the bottle top and said we would come here? I'm finding this hard to believe.' I shook my head but inside I thought he was telling the truth.

'Goldenhair gave the crown tops to the people he could trust and for ye to know who ye could trust on your journey here.' Odo placed his hand on his bony chest.

'Where is he now?' wondered Seren.

Odo crossed his legs and sat on the grass. He lowered his head and placed his hands on his knees.

'Goldenhair stayed here on the Ley Field helping me with the sheep and the cattle. He saved Nils's son from the river and ploughed the fields with the villagers. He was a kind friend to us but now the Commissioners have him and we cannot save him.'

He wiped a tear from his cheek.

'He is imprisoned with the other Whisperers - in the Castle Field.'

There were a lot of questions flying around in my mind but all I could think about was that Goldenhair could be Dad.

'I want to see him. Do you know the way?' I asked. I gestured to Seren to stand by me. ' We want to see him.'

Odo sprang to his feet.

'Alas, I cannot leave my field, it is not permitted, but I can take you to Nils and the Meadow Dwellers and they will help. Follow me!'

Without waiting, he walked on ahead at a brisk pace and never glanced back to see if we were following. We watched his spindly legs stretch out along the tall grass and his head bob up and down with the effort of walking fast.

'What do you think, Seren? Can we trust this strange little man?'

Seren held up the bottle top catching the glinting sunlight on its edges.

'We have to try. We'd better run!' she shouted as she ran off behind him. 'Wait for us! Odo, wait for us!

The Ley Field was flat ahead and soon I caught up. We were all together on our way to the Meadow Dwellers. We slowed down as we passed some large, brown cattle feeding. With their long straggly hair and huge horns, they showed no interest in us at all but their size intrigued me.

'The long haired yaks,' announced Odo reading my mind, 'They like to eat quietly.'
We came to a stop when we reached a hawthorn hedge. Odo pointed to a small gap with a wooden stile.

'Here be the start of the Meadow. Continue until ye come to three cherry trees in full blossom. Then stand near where the ground often floods and is boggy, Wait there and someone will see thee and come to thee.'

Seren waved her hand. 'Thank you, Odo,' she said politely.

I nodded, 'Err yes, thank you.'

Odo smiled and performed his peculiar dance once more before bending his knees in a bow.

'Master, Mistress, farewell, my part is done. Be of great courage.'

Before we could think of any questions, Odo sprinted sprightly back to the Ley Field and his animals.

We clambered over the stile and jumped down on to the meadow. The wide, open grassland had given way to a tilled field of crops. Rows and rows of vegetables had been planted in neat lines and it was looking like a plentiful harvest. We started along a pathway, which divided the field, and further ahead were the three cherry trees, as Odo had said. The ground next to them was marshy and had filled with enough water to cast a reflection of the trees.

'This is it. Let's rest here.'

We sat on the dusty path nearby. The sun beat down on us and I was sorry I had not taken the milk Odo had offered us.

Within minutes we could see shapes approaching, disturbing the plants on the horizon. Gradually, I realised the shapes were dogs – hounds, running and leaping over the crops. Behind them came a band of men carrying staffs. Seren clutched my arm. There was nowhere to go. If we ran they could catch us and neither of us could climb the trees.

The dogs came up to us breathing fast but instead of barking or growling at us, they greeted us like old friends - licking and bumping into us. I tickled one under the chin and Seren patted them gently along their backs.

'They're friendly,' Seren grinned. 'Are they greyhounds, Ty?'

'I think so. This one has long hair though, he's different.' I laughed as I ruffled the thick, golden fur of the largest hound.

The group of men arrived led by a tall man wearing a plaid cloak around his shoulders. He gave a shrill whistle and immediately all the dogs gathered round him, sitting patiently awaiting his instructions. He stepped forward suddenly appearing larger in our eyes. He looked down on us from his great height and bellowed.

'By whose name do you enter the meadowlands? What is your purpose trespassing here?'

I found my voice from somewhere.

'We were told to come here, to the cherry trees, by a person named Odo.'

His companions muttered to each other. The tall man fixed his eyes on me. Seren nudged me.

'Show him the bottle top!'

Slowly I removed the bottle top from my pocket and held it up.

'We have come in search of the owner of this object.'

Now Mr. Tall muttered something to his men. They nodded excitedly. His tone changed now to something softer.

'Young Master, are we permitted to know your name?'

'His name is Tyus,' announced Seren as importantly as she could, 'and I am Seren, his sister. Odo said you may be able to help us find our father.'

The giant man took a step nearer and leaned on his staff before placing one knee on the ground.

'My name is Nils, Master Tyus and Mistress Seren; it would be an honour to serve you. The Meadow Dwellers will do all we can to help you.'

His enormous face was level with us now.

'Please follow us to the village where we shall share council.'

'Do you know who is the owner of this?' I thrust the bottle top under his nose. I needed to be sure. He didn't flinch.

'Indeed, I would say the mighty Goldenhair who also entrusted me with something I must show you.'

I delved into the bag slung across his body and produced another bottle top. He smiled broadly at our mystified faces.

'Come!' He sounded the whistle and we were on our way.

The dogs set off first then Nils and his men. They led us past rows of carrots, lettuces, squash and parsnips growing heartily in the sun.

Ahead was a small collection of wooden huts covered with clay on the walls and straw on the roofs. People gathered in the centre cooking on a cauldron over an open fire. A pot of stew was keeping hot on a large stone and the tasty smell wafted towards us on the breeze. Women and children were sitting in groups and looked upon us with friendly curiosity. They were eating the stew of vegetables, which looked as delicious as it smelled. A small boy ran up to Nils. In one swoop Nils planted the boy on his shoulders. The dogs ran to their bowls for meat and drink.

'They come in search of Goldenhair.' Nils explained by way of introduction.

Everyone smiled and made room for us in the circle. Nils clicked his fingers and two bowls of stew appeared for Seren and me. A young woman with darkest eyes I'd ever seen brought it to us. She glanced down shyly as we thanked her and moved back to her place. The soup was tasty indeed and we felt revived and nourished by it. Nils stepped into the centre.

'It is time my friends. Tyus of Goldenhair has come to reclaim the deeds and free the Whisperers and we must help.'

The meadow dwellers applauded happily. Seren and I exchanged glances. Who were these Whisperers?

Nils continued solemnly. 'Here, take my staff for your quest, and for your sister...'

He handed Seren a drawstring bag made from hessian.

Seren peeped in the bag and frowned. 'Mushrooms?'

'Halt Mistress! Do not eat them or even touch them. They have much power to bring sleep and sickness.'

'No thank you,' said Seren trying to return the bag,' I don't think that's a nice gift to give anyone.'

'You must keep them. You will find a use for them.'

'Take them, Seren.' I urged noticing how serious Nils was.

'And water too for your journey.' Nils handed us leather pouches containing water.

Now I realised something. 'Aren't you coming with us Nils? We thought you would show us the way. We know nothing about your country or Whisperers.'

Nils pointed to his people.
'I don't think you understand. We are quiet meadow dwellers. We live off the land but must remain in our field at all times or the Commissioners will punish us. It is forbidden for us to leave.'

'You said you would help us.' Seren looked puzzled.

'Please do not worry Mistress, I have a helper for you that can guide you from now on.'

He whistled and the longhaired hound came bounding over.

'Rufus, stay with Tyus and Seren.' Nils whispered in the dog's ear and the animal seemed to understand. He stared keenly at us, pricking up his ears brightly.

Nils placed his bottle top on the ground, gesturing for me to do so too. Rufus sniffed at them and the area next to them as if he was tracking the scent of the owner. Then he meandered around and set off towards the hedgerows.

'Rufus has the best nose. He will lead you to Goldenhair.'

I picked up the bottle tops and put them in my hoodie.

'Come on, Seren, let's find Dad.' Taking the staff Nils had given me, I bowed a thank you. I knew it was what we had to do.

Seren took the hessian bag and waved to the meadow dwellers.

'Thank you for your help and the food.'

We could see Rufus waiting for us at the edge of the village. We ran towards him. He barked his farewell too and soon we were beyond the sight of the meadow dwellers.

4 THE SAND FIELD

Gifts from the past
For bravery now
Signal your rank
Where, when and how?

The crop planting had stopped and now the land was grassy again. No houses or buildings of any sort were to be seen. We entered a wood and wove our way through the fir trees with their familiar Christmas scent of spruce and pine. It was much cooler. The blue sky was patchy through the branches and leaves as Rufus guided us onward keeping his nose to the ground with great concentration.

'I'm getting tired. Can't we slow down?' wailed Seren.

Her orange pyjamas and her slippers appeared unsuitable for a walk in the woods but were here now - no turning back.

'We have to keep going, come on, we'll rest soon.' I half promised.

Rufus barked his encouragement and nuzzled Seren before lurching off again. We gathered up more energy and stumbled over the twigs. As the forest thinned out, more light shot through the trees.

'We're almost through.' I shouted not sure what lay outside.

Rufus barked at us to stop. We were standing at the edge of the wood and there lay immediately ahead of us, a huge drop. We stood and gaped at the rough, craggy wall, which led down to a pit. The pit must have been the size of two football pitches, covered in sand and enormous stones. This was not a beach; there was no sea, but a quarry.

Rufus led us down the loose crag with its steps of red and yellow rock slowly and skillfully until we safely reached the bottom.

'Where to now, Rufus?' Seren sighed.

In the centre of the pit was a single tower built from the rocks and slabs in the quarry and it was to here Rufus led us. It was circular with a wooden door and a look out window at the top. Rufus barked excitedly and the sound of it echoed around the quarry pit reverberating off the cliffs.

I approached the door cautiously and unlocked the door. Inside were an entrance hall and a spiral staircase.

'Hello. Anyone there?'

Silence.

Seren sat on the bottom step and took a drink from the leather pouch Nils had given her. She splashed some on Rufus to cool him. He licked her face with thanks.

I laughed and began to walk up the stairs.

'Rufus stay here with Seren. I'm going up.'

With my staff before me, I tapped my way up the spiral steps. They were made from the reddish stone from the quarry and were well worn. Someone had worked here once. I reached the top of the tower where there was a platform to view the surrounding area. There was no glass, just a breeze against my face and no Goldenhair.

On the eastern side I could see the woods we had walked through but the meadow was long out of sight. To the west was another cliff face and the sun was sinking slowly behind it. It would be night soon and it would be wise to take shelter. The whole quarry was empty and abandoned.

'There's no one here.' I shouted down the stairs turning to leave. My toe stubbed something hard.

I'd kicked an old wooden box, which was covered with dusty sand lying in the corner. Sweeping off the grains of sand with my hand, I could see there were initials carved into the wood – S. T. The lock was loose but it didn't look like it had been opened in years.

'I've found something. I'm coming down now, Seren.'

I carried the box down the steps purposefully, wondering what could be inside and why Rufus had brought us here.

'Look!' I presented the box to Seren.

'Oh, that's lovely. Whose is it?'

'I don't know but could these be our initials?' I brushed off more of the sand. ' Do you think Dad left this here for us?
Odo and Nils said Dad talked about us coming here. Maybe he left something for us in the box? I think we should open it.'

The lid lifted up easily. The first thing I saw was rolled up piece of material, which I opened out. It was a cloak made from a heavy cloth. I gave it a shake. Seren felt the shiny cloth.

'This cloak could belong to someone important, it's so grand.'

'Maybe but it's my size. It doesn't belong to a man.'

It was bronze, decorated in small circles, which merged into the fabric. I tried it on. It fitted perfectly.

'True,' Seren agreed. 'It could be made for you. What a beautiful clasp – is it gold?'

We studied the ornate, round clasp that held the cloak in place. Would a child's cloak have something so valuable?

Seren searched in the box and took out a tunic, which was smaller than the cloak and much smarter than Odo's, being made from soft, olive coloured leather.

She slipped it on over her pyjamas. Again, it was her size exactly.

'I feel like a hunter or a warrior or someone very powerful,' she mused walking about in her new garment. 'It's warm too,' she added.

'Good,' I said, 'because we'll have to rest here tonight, it's getting dark. These clothes will keep us comfortable and we can always return them.'

Seren produced a round metal disc from the pocket in the tunic.

'I don't think we are meant to after all, Ty, look it's another bottle top!'

'Dad!' we both cried. Rufus yelped in agreement.

We leant our backs against the wall and Rufus snuggled against us for extra comfort. I wrapped the cloak over us then all was darkness and black. We fell into a peaceful sleep.

5 THE YEW TREE

Light shines the way to free
If you take your chances
Beware the double danger hides
Above, between the branches.

I awoke to the sound of Rufus barking. It was still dark but the moonbeams filled the hall where we had been resting. Seren was wide-awake and standing by the door.

'Ty, I think he wants us to follow him again.'

'Oh Rufus, can't it wait till morning?' I yawned from under the cover of the cloak.

Rufus was outside kicking the sand with his paws then running in to me and shaking the grains off as he pounced on me.

'Ok, Ok, let's go. I get the message.' I said standing up.

We gathered our things and moved across the floor of the huge quarry pit in the moonlight, carefully avoiding the red slabs of stone and made our way to the cliff bottom.

Rufus did not hesitate, finding a steep path, which wound up the crag to the top. We kept him in our sights as we stretched and clambered over the loose sand and stones, grasping hold of a tuft of grass and helping each other up the vertical cliff face. Rufus stared down at us as we finally made it to the top and out of the quarry. He waited until we were safely sitting on the level grass before sniffing the air. He raised his head to the moon like a wolf and howled. Then he bounded away just as we were recovering our breath across the headland.

'Something's up ahead he wants us to see. ' Seren called.

The moon had disappeared behind a cloud so it had become much darker. I used the staff to help us follow Rufus when suddenly the cloud gave way and the bright moonlight shone on a group of large upright stones arranged in a circle.

'He's there by the stones.' I pointed with the staff.' It's like a henge in the olden days.'

The stones were eerie in the cool moonlight. I walked around them touching them with my palms, feeling the inscriptions on them in old writing.

'It's spooky,' Seren muttered, 'like a graveyard. Let's not stay here – I don't like ghosts.'

'There must be a reason Rufus brought us here, keep looking. Sing a song if you're scared.'

Seren started singing as she explored the stones.

'I'll follow the moonbeams,' she sang as she began to trace the pattern the lights made on the stones. The moonlight had cast shadows across the circle.

'Stand in the middle, Seren, what can you see?'

Seren stood in the spotlight made by the beams and tottered around slowly.

'Anything?' I asked, 'can you see anything unusual?'

Seren stopped.

'Something's glinting over there on top of that stone.'

I took my staff and reached as high as I could and swept the object off the stone. It fell to the ground with a clink.

'Where did it go?'

We spread our hands over the rough ground feeling for the object.

'Found it,' yelled Seren, holding up a gold cylinder shaped rod about 20cm long. 'What is it? What is it used for?'

I took a closer look. It appeared to be gold but with no clues on what its purpose could be.'

'Oh how I wish you could talk, Rufus.' I said aloud as Rufus sniffed the golden object in my hand.

Suddenly, Rufus growled angrily and ran off to a nearby tree, an old yew tree. He growled at the base of the tree loudly.

'Someone's up in the tree watching us!' I shouted, 'let's find out who they are.'

'No, Ty,' my sister urged, 'leave it to Rufus.'

'Here, put the rod in your pocket.' I held the staff aloft and ran towards the yew tree just as whoever it was had jumped from the branches and thrown a powdery substance over Rufus.

'Stop that! Leave our dog alone!' I yelled.

Rufus staggered round looking groggy then seemed to freeze and fall onto the ground.

'Rufus!' Seren ran over to him.

The figure turned at her voice and the light lit up his face. He had a long chin and wrinkly forehead. He was bent like a sprung coil ready to stay or run. He twisted on his heels and ran.

Rufus lay still on the ground, his fur matted with the powder the man had hurled at him.

Bending down, I started to brush the powder off him. We shook his fur and called his name softly.

'Come on boy, come on Rufus,' soothed Seren, 'here's some water.'

She poured the water over his face and Rufus stirred again. He opened his eyes but lay still. We brushed off as much of the substance as we could.

'It's alright, there you are,' I mumbled worrying about our guide and friend.

We stayed hugging him, keeping him warm in the moonlight, under the Yew Tree.

6 THE HONEY GREEN

Friendly council
Fear and flight
Creatures and nature
Aid the fight.

W e must have slept again because when I opened my eyes it was dawn and the sun was rising in line with the stones. The three of us had huddled together under my cloak. Rufus jumped up. He barked like a cockerel in a farmyard announcing a new day and he was fine once more. He trotted around the henge testing his legs.

'Who was that man spying on us last night and hurting Rufus.' Seren said crossly. 'I'd like to try feeding him the mushrooms so I would.'

'Wait a minute Seren, we don't know what harm those mushrooms can do. You were the one who said they were not a pleasant gift. Keep them safely in the pouch until an emergency.' I made sure the pouch was drawn tight.

Seren's face was reddening. 'It is an emergency. We're in a strange land and we don't know where we are going; our only friend was hurt.'

I gave her a quick hug. 'I know you're right but let's be careful and keep our eyes open.'

She brightened up and giggled now as she watched Rufus scampering amongst the henge. He came flying over to us and nuzzled both our faces before lurching off again.

'See, no harm done. He's back to full strength,' I chuckled. 'Now we have to keep up with him.'

Rufus led us past the Yew Tree and along the path the man had used for his escape. Soon we were walking briskly across another wide, open field.

'Looks like we are going west,' I said trying to sound like an explorer.'

'Oh, how clever,' giggled Seren, 'even I know the sun rises in the east so if we are walking away from the sun, we must be heading west.'

I nodded and smiled. I must remember I shouldn't underestimate my little sister.

We strolled on another hour before a dot appeared on the horizon. The dark shape became clearer as we approached. It was large wall beyond which we could see a single house like a church.

The walls of the house were made from large, grey, rectangular stones. The windows were arch shaped and the roof was thatched. Roses grew around the heavy, wooden door and flowers sprang up around the garden. A narrow path ribboned its way through the garden connecting mini houses, which were erected on the lawn – beehives.

'A beekeeper must live here,' I guessed.

'What should we do, Tyus? Should we knock at the door or wait? What if a witch lives there like in Hansel and Gretel?' Seren breathed.

'Or an ogre, ' I joined in the fright for a moment. 'No. Don't worry, they're fairy tales.' I added though I was secretly worried.

We tip toed around the house hiding from bush to bush.

'One of us should look in the window,' suggested Seren.

'You mean me.'

'Of course I mean you. I'm too small to see.'

The sun was higher in the sky. It was another clear, warm day. We had had nothing to eat and had been walking for hours. I had to do something.

Rufus was unusually quiet. Why had he brought us to this place? Our options were few.

'Right. I'm taking a peep.' I glanced at Seren curled up behind a holly bush with Rufus. They both looked tired.

Carefully, I crossed the lawn to the side of the house. I'd almost reached a window when a bell rang out like an alarm. I scrambled back to Seren and hid.

'Did they see you?' she whispered.

'What now?' I wondered. The bells continued but not like a siren wailing at all but playing a melody.

The door was thrown open and ladies appeared. They were wearing the same clothes; long, grey and white dresses and wide hats. They walked in twos with their hands tucked inside their dress pockets like a muffler. Only their faces were visible. Their eyes were fixed upon the floor and did not give the impression they were seeking an intruder. They turned the corner of the building. We watched and counted twenty.

'Shall we see where they've gone?'

Our hearts were beating fast as we took up our position by the corner of the house. The ladies were not in pairs but standing together on another lawn watching the sky and chatting. The lawn swept down to a beautiful lake.

From nowhere a flock of geese appeared flying in formation. Some landed on the lawn, others on the lake like water skiers. The geese were also grey and white with black markings on their necks. The ladies were very pleased to see them, feeding them with grain and laughing as the geese splashed into the water.
Rufus stayed close panting thirstily.

'I wonder if Rufus is quiet because he doesn't want to disturb the geese?' I whispered to Seren. 'A barking dog would surely scare them away.'

'Now that would be a remarkable dog indeed,' said a soft voice.

One of the ladies was standing behind us - she must have still been in the house after the others left.

'Hello, Rufus.' She knelt down and patted his head. Rufus licked her hand. 'Rufus has always been kind to our geese who visit us each spring.'

'You know his name!' Seren asked.

'I *do* know Rufus,' she smiled, 'but who are you and what are you doing with him?'
Before I could answer, the lady removed her hand from Rufus's back with a jolt. Some of the powder lay matted on his fur.

'Oh, Rufus, how did this happen?' Her eyes challenged us for an explanation.

It was Seren who spoke.

'A man was hiding in a tree, a yew tree and threw it on him. We tried to get most of it off.'

'Where was this?' she asked looking about the garden.

'By the stones,' Seren told her.

She nodded wisely, her eyes searching the horizon.

'Quickly, come with me, in here.'

She took hold of Rufus and brought him to a small door at the side of the house. 'Down here, it's safer here.'

I shrugged my shoulders at Seren but Seren had already decided to trust her and ran off. Down a few steps and we were in a huge kitchen and dining area under the house.

Immediately she gave Rufus some water and prepared a bowl of meat for him. She washed her hands and placed bread and cheese on a long, wooden table for us.

'Sit down, please. Eat!' She opened the cupboards and produced some delicious cakes and placed them on the table. Seren was delighted.

'Honey cakes, baked by Sister Hilda with honey from our own bees,' the mystery woman smiled.

'Come on, Ty, sit down,' commanded Seren.

As usual, I was more cautious. The lady knew Rufus and he liked her, she was concerned for him and was kind to him. She watched me hesitate.

'I will try to explain. I am the Abbess here, Abbess Julia. If I am right you have travelled from the Meadow with Rufus. You have made it through the Sand Field Stones.'

We nodded. Seren munched through the cheese hungrily.

'Then I am hopeful you are the One who is destined to rescue the Whisperers.' She stared at me.

This was sounding like a pattern. I pulled out the bottle tops to show her.

'We're searching for the person these belong to. We know nothing about Whisperers or Commissioners.'

'Shh!' She raised her hand, 'don't speak too loudly, even here. The Commissioners know you are here because the man in the tree is one of their spies. He has probably told them you have arrived so now you are in great danger. They will come for you.'

Seren's eyes filled up.

'What? What have we done?'

'Be brave child. The person you seek is imprisoned in the castle near Spring Grove. His name is Goldenhair.'

The Abbess reached into her pocket and took out a bottle top. She pressed it into my hand. I knew now we could trust her. I took a seat beside Seren.

'Tell us more,' I asked taking a honey cake.

'Goldenhair has been a great friend to us here. He showed us how to build the hives for the bees. He helped us in the church and in the garden but he was discovered. Because of his golden hair, the Commissioners thought he was the Gleaming One, the one who would take away their power and save us.'

I looked at Seren. We both shared Dad's golden hair colour. I hadn't noticed before but everyone we had met in this country had dark hair.

'It has been prophesied the Gleaming One would open the gates allowing the Whisperers to escape.'

'How many Whisperers are there?' Seren asked fiddling with her hair.

'We don't know exactly but they are also imprisoned in the castle. They are from many strange lands and have come here through tunnels and doors, caves and holes, from the past and from the future.'

'That's how we came here,' I thought.

Abbess Julia filled a bowl of water for Rufus and brushed off the remaining grains of dust.

'Each Whisperer has hair of gold and because the Commissioners thought each one could be the Gleaming One, they were arrested and put them in cells in the castle prison, trapped, unable to re-turn to their own time. So they wait and whisper to themselves longing for the real Gleaming One to come.'

'So Goldenhair is one of them?'

'Yes, he told me he was sucked here through a hole in the earth. He travelled round trying to find his way home. He helped in any way he could until the Commissioners learnt of him. We were hoping he was the One but it was not to be.'

She sighed a long sigh.

'But you young sir, I believe you may be the Gleaming One.'

'No, I'm not,' I protested, ' I came through a tunnel like the others, with my sister.'

'Yes, but you wear the cloak of authority and the stones spoke to you. Did they give you anything?'

I nodded.

'Good. It is happening. We always thought the prophesy meant one but it may mean two.' She turned to Seren. 'You, my dear may have to play a part.'

Seren gulped.

'Once the Whisperers are released, the Commissioners' power will cease and they will have to leave, allowing us to live in peace once more. We will be able to see one another again, speak to our friends in other fields. For many years we have been confined to our own houses. I haven't seen the Meadow Dwellers and my other friends for many years.'

She clasped her hands together.

'It is wonderful you are here but you have to get to the Castle Field.'

Seren's eyes grew wider. 'But we're children. How can we tell the Commissioners what to do? I'm sure they have soldiers at a castle and they have spies with powder that causes you to freeze up and lots more I bet.'

'Yes, but you have the golden key, golden hair and the prophesy.'

Loud cackling interrupted our conversation. The geese were upset, flapping and flying everywhere. The sisters were looking perplexed running after them and trying to calm them down with grain and seeds.

'Someone's coming,' Abbess Julia said hearing the commotion, 'the geese are alarmed. Come!'

She put some honey cakes in one bag and some bones for Rufus in another.

'Whether you are the One or not, you must journey on for the Commissioners are riding this way and they will imprison you and you will become another Whisperer. Your only chance is to rescue the Whisperers and Goldenhair. Then you will know if you are the One.'

'I'm scared.' Seren bleated.

'No we're not Seren.' I gave her my best confident smile even though I was shaking inside. "We are going to rescue Dad, come on!'

'This way.' The Abbess led us up the stone steps to the back of the church where the other sisters and geese were flailing around. Everyone stopped in surprise when we appeared.

The drumming of the approaching horses' hooves made the ground under our feet shudder. The Abbess pointed to the water.

'You must cross the lake and take the way down the Deys Brook. It will take you to the castle. Stay on the Deys Brook.'

Now the sound of the Commissioners' horses grew louder. They thundered towards the church house, unsettling the geese, which honked and hissed.

'The Commissioners are coming', the sisters cried.

The Abbess dragged a small, round boat from the rushes.

'Get in the coracle!' she ordered.

Rufus jumped in to the craft and lay his paw across Seren while I tried to row. I had kayaked at camp so I had some practice but how far could I get before the Commissioners were upon us? I could see them clearly, dressed in long, black, billowing cloaks riding fiercely towards us.

There were a dozen or so riders kicking up the soil as they trampled over the garden, knocking over the beehives and destroying the flowers. They were coming after us and not going to stop at the lake. I was sure they would catch us.

The sisters hurried out of the way of the galloping horses, picking up the squawking geese that hadn't flown to the safety of the skies.

We pushed off. I was surprised how quickly we moved, the lake seemed to be helping. We were far from the shore in no time but the Commissioners had dismounted and searching for boats to follow us.

'Come on, Seren, take an oar,' I gasped, 'Two is better than one.

7 THE DEYS BROOK

Myth and mire
Choices made
Take you under
Or take you higher.

Seren turned to take a paddle from under the wooden seat. I was frantically rowing, splashing the sides as I oared one side then the other. She called out above the spray.

'Look, Ty, look! There's a mist coming down on the shore. It's covering the house, the geese, everything. I can't see the Commissioners anymore.'

I panted to a stop and scanned the shore – a thick, shimmering mist obscured the view. Dark shapes were zigzagging under the misty cloud, shouting and shrieking.

'It's not a mist. I think that cloud is hundreds of bees swarming around. Listen!'

Sure enough there was a continuous hum as the bees buzzed around, stinging and irritating the Commissioners. The bees were not happy their hives had been damaged.

'They'll never catch us now,' cried Seren.

We paddled a while longer until we reached the bank on the far side of the lake. A narrow brook fed into the lake.

'This must be the Deys Brook. We will have to row upstream now so it might be more difficult,' I guessed.

Silently, saving our energy, we carried on rowing up the stream, watching it babble against us. It was harder work than the lake. Seren wiped her brow.

'How far do we go? Aren't we safe yet?'

'Abbess Julia said this will lead to the castle so we have to keep going.' I answered. My arms were aching and I wanted to rest too.

Rufus, who had been lying still throughout our escape, stood up and picked his way to the front of the coracle and barked. His big eyes stared at me.

'He wants us to stop here, I think.'

We pulled over to the bank. Rufus jumped out. Seren and I carefully followed him. I dragged the coracle on to the riverbank, watching the brook trickling back down towards the lake. If the Commissioners were pursuing us we would have to be quick.

I hid the coracle under a bush and covered it with branches and leaves. Seren found some large pieces of moss and bracken for the sides.

'If they come after us, they won't see where we've landed and might carry on up stream.'

Seren stretched her arms to the sky.

'Do you believe everything the Abbess said, Ty?' She smoothed down the leather tunic wiping away the twigs and leaves that were stuck to the fabric.

'Have we travelled back in time or is this some in between land that has been stuck – frozen?'

'Like a glitch in time - like on a screen?' I added.

She looked more serious. 'And are you the Gleaming One who has come to fix it?'

I laughed. It was odd like so much that had happened recently.

'I don't know – but I do know one of the Whisperers is Dad and he has been here with these people and now he is in prison so we have to go on.'

'Right then, shall we walk? It's too hard to row up the stream,' she suggested.

'If we follow the stream but walk next to it, taking its route, it can still lead us to the castle. We can walk faster than we can row. We'll stay by the trees.' I agreed.

Staying close to each other and with Rufus sniffing the way ahead, we stayed by the cover of the trees. We were on alert for spies in the branches or Commissioners coming up behind. Through the gaps in the fronds, the geese were flying above circling the woods and the Deys Brook.

The Deys Brook route weaved ahead. It took a sharp turn on to a plain where two crossing bridges divided the land. There were a few steps either side. The high, wavy grass on this part of the land was wild and in flower. It looked difficult to wade through but passable.

'If we cross the bridges, it will save time and cut out a long walk,' I ventured impetuously.

I ran towards the first bridge. It was old and rickety. Rufus barked excitedly. I was halfway across already.

'It's OK, Rufus, it's solid enough.'

I jumped from the last step on to the grass and rushed ahead, sweeping the grass aside with my staff. Rufus was barking louder. He stood on the bridge not allowing Seren to pass.

'Come back, Ty!' I heard her voice above the swooshing of the tall grass.

I was nearing the next bridge when suddenly; the ground became marshy and boggy. My feet were sinking. I was up to my ankles in water. It was difficult to make progress through the soppy mud.

Who would build bridges that would take you on to unsafe ground? It doesn't make sense. If the land floods between the bridges wouldn't it be wiser to make a longer bridge? The ground was wetter and colder. I was sinking up to my knees now. I could hear Seren shouting but couldn't hear what she was saying. I glimpsed her and Rufus on the bridge.

'Stay there! The land is a swamp. It's dangerous.' I cried.

I wondered if I could leap on to the second bridge? My saturated feet were stuck, heavy as concrete. I brought up my staff to try the ground to lever myself forward. The staff half disappeared into the earth; I couldn't wedge it out.

Feeling scared, I wondered why I had taken a stupid risk. I was the careful one, the watcher. Why didn't I wait? Even if I could lift the staff, how could I get myself out? I can't fly. I took a breath and tried to be calm. I wasn't sinking any further but I couldn't move. How can I make it back to Seren? I could barely turn. I was shivering uncontrollably as the cold crept up my legs.

Then I felt myself being lifted out of the mire and into the air. Something had forced itself under my body and raised me up on a spike. It was warm and hairy like a dog but it wasn't Rufus. No, its head was like a large goat or antelope. Its enormous, long antlers had skewered me, catching my clothes and lifting me high above the ground. It swiveled me this way and that, like I was on a crazy, fairground ride.

The peculiar creature carried me towards Seren on the bridge. Its hooves sploshed heavily as it tore through the bog. It held me aloft so I could see above the grass. There were more of them – at least ten and they followed my rescuer with their sharp antlers pointing to the sky.

The large, hairy goat-dog swung me onto the bridge like a puppet, unhinged me so I dropped onto the wooden planks.

'No man can cross here,' its gravelly voice announced. 'Man must stay on the Deys Brook. The plain and the marshes belong to us – The Yales.'

44

I watched his mouth moving; fangs bright and white churned out the words but this beast was my rescuer.

'I'm sorry,' I murmured, 'Thank you for saving me. We are not from your land and we were only trying to reach the castle.'

The other Yales drew closer and stood around the bridge. The leader stamped his hoof. Rufus gave a short bark and crouched down. Seren patted him gently.

'It's true Mr. Yale,' she started, 'we are lost. We don't have a map. We thought it would be quicker to cross here.'

The Yale's ochre eyes studied her carefully.

'You have entered uncharted land and have fallen into the trap of the two bridges. These are false crossings placed there by the Commissioners. Foolish man – seeking to take the easy route will always fail.'

The other Yales lurched to and fro at his words, knocking into each other and nodding. The leader Yale raised his head.

'Many have perished here. Today you had good fortune because we were grazing nearby. Even so, although it is forbidden to assist trespassers, I could not let you perish.'

I swallowed my tears. I had not realised how close I had come to danger. 'I'm so sorry and again, thank you so much.' I uttered blinking my eyes and feeling foolish.

It didn't matter that I was talking to an annoyed antelope. It was silly of me to cut corners and maybe lead all of us into peril.

'We will keep to the path close to the Deys Brook.' I vowed. 'Come Seren, let's be going. We must find the Castle.'

We edged along the bridge and back on to the pathway.

'Wait!' the large Yale ordered. 'The Castle field is beyond the Deys Brook, where it meets the Alt River. Take that path up onto the high ridge!' He swiveled his antlers and pointed to a steep incline ahead.

One of the other Yales held my staff in his antlers and trotted up to the bridge. The leader recognised it at once.

'This staff belongs to the Meadow Dwellers – how do you come by it and why are you travelling to the Castle?'

'Nils gave it me as a gift to help us on our quest to find the man who owns this.' I showed him the bottle top. 'We believe he is being held at the Castle.'

'And we are going to rescue him,' chimed in Seren. 'We think he might be our father.'

The Yale roared laughing.

'You have spirit young daughter but there are dangers to be faced.' He gave her a lob sided smile.

He nodded to the Yale who held my staff. He threw the staff towards me, landing at my feet. I picked it up and bowed a thank you.

'You will need the staff,' the Yale turned to me, ' and you will need more good fortune and better choices if you seek that person.'

'Thank you for helping us.' I repeated grasping my staff. It felt good to hold it again.

'Be gone, now,' the Yale turned to leave.

'I wish you could come with us,' smiled Seren who had taken to the Yale. His features softened somehow.

'Alas, we cannot cross from the land between the bridges, only a Whisperer can do so.'

'Are we Whisperers then?' gasped Seren.

'My dear, you are the Queen of the Whisperers.'

8 THE BLACK MOOR MOSS

If advice and knowledge
be scorned on the path
Then the quest is clouded
with doubt and wrath.

T he Yale spun on his hooves and left us. He led his herd through the reeds, each one sinking slowly, becoming hidden as their antlers submerged beneath the grass until they could no longer be seen.

We stood still a moment. I started shivering again.

'Well, did you hear that? He said I was a queen! What do you think, Tyus? Do you think I am a queen?' Seren laughed.

I stormed off with Rufus onto the path.

'Ty,' she called, 'I'm a queen.'

'All right, your majesty,' I scoffed, 'but get moving. We've got to make it to the ridge.'

'Queen Seren,' she chuckled as she caught us up. She could be annoying sometimes.

I squelched up to the ridge, still soaking and smelling of the damp marshes. The bottom of my cloak was muddy and the ditchwater seeped up the material along my back. I forced myself up to the ridge trying to get further away from the Two Bridges and the memory of my mistake.

We reached the top and first took in the view behind us. The trees we had walked through when we abandoned the coracle, the Deys Brook, the bridges and the land between them where the Yale lived, all in sight but before us lay a different landscape. Beyond was dark, vast moorland – no trees or hills – an expanse of featureless dusty, black moss.

We sat on the ridge and rested. Seren remembered the honey cakes she had in her bag and shared them between the three of us.

'The Abbess said follow the Deys Brook,' she said munching the cakes.

'And the Yale said this is the best route,' I replied, 'and he did save my life.' I nibbled away at the honey cake.

'It's very strange but I feel I belong here somehow. After all if I am queen,' Seren teased, ' maybe you are king.'

'Never!' I mocked, 'Queen of Whisperers! You have never whispered in your life – ever. You are the loudest, noisiest, most annoying sister...'

I was only getting started when Seren grabbed my hand firmly. She put her finger on my lips.

'Shh! Over there!' she finally spoke in a whisper.

Looking over the ridge were the horsemen who had tried to capture us at the abbey convent. They galloped furiously through clouds of dust across the moor. Commissioners! Their faces were unclear but their long, silky, black cloaks swelled out behind them. They were tearing across the black landscape, black on black as if they were fleeing a monster.

'So, the Commissioners are on their way to the Castle.' I guessed.

'Why aren't they looking for us?' wondered Seren.

'I don't know. Maybe they think we have drowned in the lake or become trapped in the swamp. Perhaps we are not important anymore.'

The dust cloud disappeared into the distance. The Commissioners were out of sight. Seren sat up straight with her serious face on.

'What are we going to do at the Castle – if we get there? We can't fight the Commissioners. Everyone is scared of them – the Meadow Dwellers, the Sisters, even the Yale. All are trapped in their zones.

They lock up the Whisperers in the castle prison and if we go there that's what they'll do to us. We're just two kids. I'm not really a queen and you're not really a warrior. We stand no chance!' Tears filled Seren's eyes.

'Now, don't cry.' I pleaded.

I tried to think of words to say but all I saw was my sister, my frail, little sister, the one who walks in her sleep that we have to protect, vulnerable and pathetic, looking up at me, so I hugged her close and said nothing.

Rufus licked my hands and nuzzled Seren's neck, whining a sad song. I broke free and stamped about the ridge.

Was it impossible? I tried to formulate an answer – a plan.

'I suppose I thought we'd get to the Castle and Dad would take charge. I never thought how we would break in and help him escape.'

The dust from the moor caught me in the eye. I rubbed it as it started to water and itch. I sat quietly for a moment while my eye reddened with the grit. Then my thoughts began to run. This started because of a stupid, bottle top that could have belonged to anyone. Why would Goldenhair, as they call him, be our Dad? Dad went off that's what happened. He didn't come to some fanciful land with strange creatures and people who look like they are from the past. It's ridiculous!

I looked across the moor – there was nothing but emptiness. The Commissioners had vanished and the notion of having to cross the vast black field by foot was not appealing. The Commissioners had been on horseback, travelling fast. It must be miles across.

The next part of the journey could take us hours. I was debating whether or not we should turn back. Seren was tired and upset, I was soaking wet and now a cold breeze drifted in from the moor. The black, dusty ground could be another trap. The wind gusted against us, almost pushing us down onto the mossy moor.

'I'm cold, Tyus,' Seren sighed, 'May I borrow your cloak?'

She pulled it towards her with a mighty tug breaking the golden buckle. It rolled off onto her lap.

'Oh no, I'm sorry, Ty, it just broke off.' Seren breathed.

'You mean you pulled it off when you dragged it off my shoulders,' I yelled sharply. 'You needn't have used such force.'

I have never spoken so gruffly to Seren before and I could see she was apologizing but it didn't matter, I couldn't stop. My eye was hurting and my clothes were damp.

'Sorry. I didn't mean to. I'd never break it on purpose. Let's share the cloak.' She undid the buckle. 'I might be able to fix the clasp. Let me try.'

'No! You've done enough. Here you can have it!' I threw the cloak towards her and stamped off down the slope onto the moor. 'And why don't you go back home!' I added meanly.

I didn't look back. If she wanted to follow that was up to her. I can't be looking after her all the time.

Bewildered, Seren remained at the ridge top watching me disappear across the moor and its darkness.

She picked up the buckle to put into her bag with the cakes and the gold cylinder shaped rod we had found at the Sand Field Stones. Clutching the heavy cloak around her, she slid awkwardly down the slope after me.

I thought I could hear her calling my name but the wind was up and whirling the dust about. My eye felt gritty and sore as more specks caught in my face blown by the wild wind.

I'd walked about a hundred metres and I knew there must be thousands more to go. Inside I was hoping Seren had found her way to the beginning, through the tunnel and back home. I wouldn't have to look out for her then. I can do this. I am older. I am stronger. I'm the hero – not her!

Thoughts of Seren being a queen or more important in the rescue bubbled up inside my head. She was the one who led me here so I could rescue Dad. She's a baby holding me back now. She should go home.

I trudged further. There was another cry on the wind. 'Ty-us!'

Seren's voice was cutting though the wind and the dust.

'Oh no, go home Seren. Don't come after me.'

I stuck my staff into the ground and waited. The voice didn't sound any nearer; in fact, it was disappearing further into the dark.'

I felt completely alone in the wilderness. My stomach tightened and from deep inside I yelled her name.

'Seren!'

Not because I was scared for me but because I was scared for her. I snapped back from the dark cloud that was trying to engulf me.

'Seren!'

My sister lost on the black moor moss searching for me. I'd left her because I was cross and angry about buckles and jealous because the Yale declared her queen while I was the reckless brother who got stuck in the boggy quicksand.

Perhaps I am not as clever as I thought. The only time I got into real trouble was when I went off on my own. Here I am making the same mistake again. Seren needs me and I need her.

Now my thoughts began to gel. Seren was the one who trusted Odo and the Meadow Dwellers, who understood Rufus, who believed Abbess Julia. She was the one who was with Dad when he disappeared.

It was Seren the Commissioners really wanted! She is the key to everything. Seren!

'Tyus.' Her voice was not too far.

'Tyus,' she called again.

I made my way towards her voice until I saw her shape huddled with Rufus under the cloak. All at once the wind dropped.

'Seren, I'm so sorry, 'I've messed up. I shouldn't have shouted.'

Now I was almost in tears. The itchiness in my eyes had gone, washed out by the water. I wiped away the last piece of grit.

'It's OK, Ty, we're together again and I've got something to show you.

9 THE CASTLE

Risk and revenge
Creatures save and aid
But put in jeopardy
The plans that were made.

S eren removed her hand from her bag. She was holding the
buckle and the metal rod. She pushed the rod into a space
on the buckle.

'The two pieces fit perfectly together. What does it look like to
you now?' she quizzed.

I took hold of the new creation and smiled.

'Exactly! It's a key!' I was astonished.

I felt the heavy weight in my hand. The golden buckle and golden
rod were united.

'I suspect it will come in useful at the Castle,' Seren smiled
warmly.

'How did you work it out?' I asked.

'I don't know. I looked at them and remembered something the
Abbess said before we had to escape – *you have the golden key* – then
I tried them together.'

She put the key safely in the bag and tightened the drawstring.

Rufus bounded towards us, shaking off the dust from the moor.

'Hey! Steady! We're dirty enough.' I rubbed his fur and hugged
him.

Warmth came back into me. 'I'm sorry I left you too, old boy. I won't leave either of you again.'

Rufus rolled over and licked my hand with his pink tongue.

Taking off the cloak, I shook the remaining dirt from it. It felt dry with no damage as far as I could see. As I spread it out to inspect it further, loud cackling noises filled the air. We looked to the sky to see the geese flying towards us in formation.

The lead goose spotted us below, changed direction and swooped down, landing gracefully beside us. They trotted around us pecking at the ground and flapping their wings.

'Why are they here?' I wondered.

'Maybe the Abbess sent them,' said Seren. 'We saw them when we hid the coracle. Could they have been searching for us all this time?'

If Seren was right, the geese may have noticed we left the Deys Brook and wanted to warn us about the danger of the two bridges and the black moor. Although it was hard we should have continued to row up the stream as we were advised.

I stepped aside. 'Let's see what they do.'

The geese waddled in circles for a while but gradually they surrounded the cloak I had spread out upon the ground. Each goose took a piece of cloth in its mouth and lifted the cloak into the air as we watched mesmerized. They held the cloak firmly making patterns in the sky, then brought it down to earth gently laying it at our feet.

Seren leaped in the air, clapping her hands at their cleverness.

'Ouch!' I felt a nudge behind me. Several of the geese were pushing me onto the cloak. 'Shall I wear my cloak friends?'

Seren and Rufus were also being shepherded towards the cloak.

Some geese were cackling louder. What were they trying to do?

Rufus realised first. He jumped onto the cloak and curled up as if ready to sleep. Seren sat next to him, legs crossed, arms round Rufus's neck.

A few geese corralled me on to the cloak too. I scrunched up beside Seren and waited. Seren was giggling like her usual self.

'They'll never do it, Seren – it's impossible.'

Seren squeezed my arm and giggled. 'Hold tight, I think they are going to try.'

We watched open mouthed as the geese took hold of the edges of the cloak once more. We sat very still while they stretched out the cloak and fluttered above the land. Within seconds we were airborne, floating high above the black moor and the ridge.

Immediately, I felt so much better. The feelings of doubt and anger disappeared. Seren's face was a picture of calm. Her eyes scanned the horizon for the castle, clutching on to Rufus as we sped through wisps of cloud.

The draining black moor trailed behind us. It had had a bad effect on us, me in particular. Maybe that was why the Commissioners rode so quickly across it – before its power brought them down and tore their spirit.

As we neared our destination, the geese slowly descended so we could see the Castle.

The timber fort stood atop a hill. A tall, square tower commanded the centre, several stories high. A flag was raised, blowing in the breeze. Soldiers stood outside the heavy entrance door. The outer walls were well protected by bowman. At the bottom of the hill were huts for people and animal pens. The two parts were surrounded by water with a moat and drawbridge connecting them. They did not foresee an attack coming from the sky!

'The tower must be the Castle prison,' Seren decided, 'it looks the most protected. That must be where the Whisperers are being held.'

My gaze, however, was fixed on one of the people on the ground. He stared directly back at me as we flew lower and he recognised me! He was as surprised as me to see geese flying two children and a dog on a cloak.

It was the man who was hiding in the tree by the Sand Field Stones, the one who had hurt Rufus with the mystery powder. He started running towards the castle, yelling and waving his arms about.

'We've been spotted,' I called, 'we have to be quick.'

The geese swept low setting us down behind the prison tower out of sight of the guards. We stayed close to the fort watching as the geese scattered into the air.

They circled above the tower and the walls, diving down and pecking the bowmen on the fortress. The archers took their bows and aimed at the geese but the geese were too fast for them, avoiding every arrow but they were taking a great risk for us. They could easily have flown away from danger.

Everyone was looking at the sky. No one had noticed us. This was our chance. The soldiers guarding the door moved away, distracted by the unusual target practice of their fellow guards. They laughed at the poor performance of the bowmen as the geese soared higher away from the arrows. They teased them and called jibes at them. This was sport indeed.

The coast was clear. Moving forward, I tried the round handle on the prison door. It was locked.

Seren took out the golden key.

'Try it,' she mouthed at me.

I tried the keyhole. It turned. This time the handle clicked open. I pushed the door just wide enough for us to squeeze through. Glancing back, I saw the geese were still amusing themselves with the guards.

I followed Seren and Rufus into the tower and shut the door. A gloomy light fell on a staircase that led up to the different floors of the tower. There was a smell of damp, stale air and straw. Luckily, it was unguarded.

'This must be where they keep the Whisperers, it's horrible,' I gasped.

I pulled back the first door on the ground floor. Inside were two cages on either side of the dungeon, each holding a man. They shrieked when they saw us and ran to the bars shaking them. One had dirty, yellow hair and pale, paper like skin; the other was older with long, white hair and dingy teeth. They were whispering something hoarsely that was hard to understand. I hushed them.

'Shh! The guards will hear. Do you know Goldenhair? Where is Goldenhair?'

The first man squinted at me and pointed to the ceiling. He was upstairs. I wanted to help them but we had to get to Dad first. They continued their soft whispering.

I shut the door. Rufus ran up the stairs ahead of us to the next floor and another door. Again we could hear whispering from behind the door.

'More prisoners,' I said sadly.

'More Whisperers, I think,' said Seren, 'Where is Dad, Rufus?'

She put a bottle top under his nose. He got the scent at once and leapt up the stairs again until he could go no higher. He growled at the door as we approached breathlessly behind him. From the bottom of the tower came banging and shouting.

'Soldiers! Commissioners! They're opening the main door, they are coming.' I cried.

We could hear them searching the ground floor cells. Rufus was pawing at the door now. Dad must be in here. I opened the door slowly. Through the dark I could see a man with his back turned but he had Dad's fair hair.

'Goldenhair?' I uttered.

He turned into the light. His kindly face was the same as always.

"Dad!' yelled Seren, 'It's Dad!'

'Tyus! Seren! You're here? I knew you would come.'

He reached through the bars and took our hands. The sounds of the guards wafted up the stairs.

'You have to get out of here.' Dad said with a worried brow.

"Not without you, Dad,' said Seren.

I took the golden key and found the lock, twisting it many times but it wouldn't catch to unlock.

'Hide!' said Dad, 'don't worry about me. The guards will be here soon.'

'Let me try,' Seren took the key and tried again. The lock sprung open.

Dad opened the door and hugged us. For a moment everything froze. It didn't matter about the guards or the danger we were in. We had our Dad back and he was hugging us.

'Hide behind the door!' he ordered.

We crouched behind the door as the first guard came in. Dad had gone back into the cage and pretended nothing had happened. He was whispering something over and over like the other men. The guard seemed content the prisoner was still there and didn't see us. But then another man entered and this was too much for Rufus. It was the tree man!

Rufus could see his chance for revenge. He growled viciously and hurtled towards the man in an attempt to bite his leg. The guard was fighting him off with a sword and the commotion now brought the other guards running.

I took my staff and tripped up the guard with the sword. Two of the other guards grabbed hold of me easily. Dad came charging out of the cell to try to rescue me but there were too many of them. They pinned our arms behind our backs. Rufus was tied with string and was about to be led away. Had we come all this way for nothing?

Seren stepped from the shadows. Calmly, she took the bag of mushrooms Nils had given her and threw them up into the air.

'Stop. Release them!' she boomed.

The mushrooms exploded in the air showering the guards and the tree man in silvery dust. They fell to the ground, motionless, overcome by the mysterious mushroom powder.

'Untie us, Seren,' yelled Dad as Seren stood there in shock.

Dad released Rufus while Seren untied me.

'Come on, let's get out of here.' Dad insisted, 'well done Seren that was a brave thing to do.'

We started down the steps passed the sleepy guards.

'Seren, do you have the golden key? Will you unlock the cages of the other prisoners? These people are innocent of any crimes like me.'

Seren unlocked each cage and one by one, the old Whisperers followed us to the bottom of the tower. The door was closed. Dad raised his arm to stop everyone. He opened the heavy door allowing sunlight into the gloom.

'It's clear – come before the guards recover and follow us.'

Rufus led the way, staying close to the cover of the tower, sliding down the muddy hill, through the dried up part of the moat and back into the cover of the trees and undergrowth.

No one spoke. Rufus and Dad leading, Seren and I close behind with the other Whisperers trotting far behind us at the rear, unsteadily on their feet and squinting as they became used to sunlight once more.

'Where are we going, Dad?' my voice broke through the tense silence. 'They're going to come after us.'

'Not far to go now, Tyus. If we are quick, we can make it to the Spring Grove before they find us.' Dad plodded on through the wood.

The Whisperers caught up to us, breathing heavily and whispering as they had been in their cages, only now I could understand their words. I realised what they had been repeating while they were locked away.

Spring Grove! Spring Grove! SPRING GROVE!

10 SPRING GROVE

Falling pink and white
The glow and the gleam
Wisdom of innocence
The end of the dream

T he wooded area gave way to rows of spaced out fruit trees filled with blossom. In the middle, almond trees had been planted in a circle and were with laden with fragrant pink and white flowers.

'The Grove!' announced Dad.

'It's beautiful,' said Seren.

Rufus kicked up the soil beneath the tree trunks where the grass had not grown.

I needed answers. 'What happens now, Dad? How do we get home?'

Dad smiled at me then drew me towards him. 'I'm so proud of you both.'

The Whisperers reached the grove and fell on to the grainy soil exhausted. The Commissioners were not following yet as far as we could see.

'And what did you mean when you said you knew we would come?'

Dad took a deep breath. 'It's along story, Tyus, but I knew the Commissioners would come for you and Seren once they realised I wasn't the Gleaming One.'

Hearing her name, Seren stepped over to join us. He pointed to the Whisperers sitting beneath the almond trees.

'Each one of these men has been taken from his true time by

the Commissioners – from different centuries and countries – and brought here to this place just like me. You see the Commissioners have been searching for someone, who it has been foretold, will conquer them and give the inhabitants their freedom back. Freedom to live together in harmony, to travel, to work and share again as they did long ago. Someone named the Gleaming One.

When they discovered they had captured the wrong person they locked us up in the Castle knowing that one day the Gleaming One would attempt to rescue us and they could capture him. All we knew was that the Spring Grove was important and so we wouldn't forget, we have been whispering the name over and over.

The day they took me, they were so close to capturing the real Gleaming One. They made a mistake, they took the wrong person.'

My stomach was filled with butterflies. 'You mean Seren! They wanted Seren!'

Seren stood tall. Her tunic glowed under the blossom trees. 'Me?' she said.

'Yes Seren,' Dad said, 'And Tyus too. You are the ones with the power. Some people give out a little power, like these men and me too which the Commissioners could sense. Tyus has more but you, Seren, you have great power.'

'The Yale said I was Queen of the Whisperers.'

'It's true,' continued Dad. 'Once they realised their mistake they have been trying to lure you here. I gave my bottle tops to people I could trust so you would know you were on the right track. I hoped Tyus would remember them as you were so small when I was taken.'

'I did Dad. I knew it was you from the moment I saw them.' I said.

Dad knelt up and checked to see if it was still safe.

'The Commissioners have controlled this land for centuries. We have to help these people take back their lives.'

"But how?' asked Seren, 'I don't know how to use this power.'

'You do,' I said, 'Remember Odo, the mushrooms, the Yales. You were always the wise one. You knew who to trust.'

'Yes,' said Dad, 'and when the time comes you will know what to do.'

'But why are we here in Spring Grove?' she asked.

'Is there a spring here?' I ventured, 'Like a stream and we can float back to the tunnel.'

We looked about quickly realising there was no spring.

'Then what is a grove?' Seren asked.

'It's a collection of trees,' answered Dad. 'Let's see what is so special about them.'

We touched the rough bark on each tree, stood under the heavy blossom on the branches as they cast a pink glow on our faces. We walked up and down the rows and round the inner circle of the trees. Rufus scratched on the bark causing the blossom to fall.

'Careful Rufus, you're disturbing the blossom,' I chided but Rufus continued until more and more blossom fell.

'That's it! Rufus always knows,' said Seren.

She started tapping at one of the trees until the blossom fell like a snowfall, 'Everyone come on, shake, tap, scratch the trees!'

The old Whisperers joined us beating against the trunks until the blossom fell thick and fast on to the soil and it was difficult to see each other.

'Keep going!' cried Seren.

The blossom was covering our feet and ankles yet the branches were still full. The blossom cascaded over us.

'Something weird is happening,' I heard myself say as the blossom was thundering above our heads.

'No,' said Dad, 'Listen! It's the Commissioners, they're on their way here!'

The other Whisperers began to cover themselves in the blossom that had fallen so they couldn't be seen. Dad started covering up Seren and me but Seren stopped him.

'No Dad, we can't keep running and hiding or they will always keep coming after us. We have to stay and face them. We can't fight them though, we're only children.'

Dad stared at the forest. The Commissioners were visible now in their inky cloaks riding through the trees. They would soon be here.

'Seren is right,' said Dad, 'we will face them. And you are not just children; you are the Gleaming Ones. We'll do this together.'

I took my staff and planted my feet. Seren stood beside Rufus. Dad went to the edge of the grove and waited. The trees had stopped vibrating but there was enough blossom on the ground to hide like the Whisperers if necessary. Then the Commissioners appeared at the Grove.

They stopped when they saw us, unsure what to do. All these years they had been expecting a man of great power not two children. Rufus snarled a greeting. Their horses responded with a snort.

The Commissioners drew back their cloaks to reveal their bows across their bodies. They each took a quiver and took aim.

'Wait!' cried Dad. 'You can't do that, it's wrong and ungallant. We are unarmed. Allow us to return to our own time and we will leave you alone.'

They held their rock like pose a moment longer.

'Put down your weapons. Would noble warriors fight with children?'

One or two of the Commissioners put down their arrows, slowly followed by the rest of them.

'Now we will return to our homelands and never come here again,' Dad said.

'No Dad,' Seren stepped forward. ' It is not their land. We cannot leave unless they allow the Meadow Dwellers and the Sisters and the Yale to be free.'

'Shh, little Seren,' Dad hushed but it was too late. I had to speak also.

'She's right. You have been waiting for the Gleaming One to come. You thought the Gleaming One would destroy you so you searched the centuries to silence them by imprisoning them in your land where you rule with fear and unfairness.'

'Shh, Tyus,' I heard Dad say. 'They're children, they don't know what they're talking about.'

The Commissioners raised their bows again but I found the courage to continue.

'Let me finish. The Gleaming One was in the prophecy so you knew this day was always going to happen. You must listen, it has been foretold.'

The leader raised his hand and they put down their bows once more. He folded his arms ready to listen.

The blossom rustled and the Whisperers appeared, rising up from their blossom beds and gathering round Seren. Rufus took his position of protection in front of her. Seren glowed as the sunlight bounced from the blossom onto her face. She pointed to the sky. The geese were flying above them. Everyone waited. Then Seren spoke.

'There will be a meeting of all the people who live here. You, the Meadow Dwellers, the herdsmen, the Abbess and the Sisters, the Yale and you will talk, not fight.

You will listen to each other and you will change and learn and learn to live together or the black moor moss will grow larger and fill everyone with doubt, sadness and anger. The crops will fail and the river will flood, the bees will stop making honey and the geese will fly away never to return. Everyone is needed and must be valued.

This is what I have come to say and you must believe it is true for your own happiness as well as others.'

The Commissioners looked worried, their faces tired with the fight. Their leader dismounted and walked towards Seren transfixed by her words. From the edge of the wood came the leader of the Yale, Abbess Julia and Nils, followed by a skipping Odo. They had left their enclosures for the first time having been drawn here by Seren and the magical blossom. They stood together on the carpet of flowers. The Commissioner put down his bow and joined them. They joined hands and raised them high then knelt together, spellbound by Seren's words.

'We shall do as you command, O Gleaming One,' they chanted as one. Then they embraced each other and shook hands.

'Now we must go,' Seren said.

She knelt down and patted Rufus. 'It is hard to leave you Rufus but we have to return to our own time and families. You are needed here.'

Rufus nuzzled her hand and I stroked his golden fur one last time. Nils signaled to him and off he ran.

'Come we are going home,' announced Dad.

How? I wondered.

The Whisperers moved into the centre of the grove where the almond tree blossom was luxuriously thick. Dad, Seren and I joined them. The ground began to shake and the blossom began to shower us again with flakes of delicate pink and white petals.

The Commissioners, Abbess, Nils, the Meadow Dweller, the Yale and Odo moved away in awe of what was happening.

'Here, stand close Whisperers!' cried Seren.

The trees shook violently and the blossom reigned down covering our shoulders in their magic. Then, there was a ping!

The oldest white haired whisperer flew into the air and disappeared. Then another – ping! And another! Ping! Ping!

'Spring Grove! Spring Grove! Spring Grove!" they shouted.

'They have gone back to their time,' said Dad.

Ping! Dad was next to go, leaving just Seren and me.

'It should be me next, then you,' Seren cried squeezing my hand. 'You were the last to come here so you will be the last to leave.'

The Abbess and Odo smiled and waved. 'Thank you, Master and Mistress!'

Nils held on to Rufus, the Yale pounded his hoof in salute. The Commissioners were terrified, wrapping their cloaks around their bodies' tight. The ground rumbled again and with an avalanche of blossom and a ping, Seren flew up and disappeared.

I waited for my turn. The trees were glowing. I heard the geese in the sky. Rufus barked one bark of farewell, then ping! I was lifted up.

I don't remember anything else but I came to in the pantry in the

Mill house. Seren was there. I was a bit dazed but she hugged me tightly.

'Are we home? Are we safe?' I asked.

'Yes, we're home.' Seren smiled.

I looked around the pantry. There was no sign of the secret trap door that led to the tunnel and the past. Seren's doll lay propped up against the wall waiting for her owner patiently.

Footsteps approaching from the room outside startled us but then we heard Mum's voice. She opened the pantry door.

'Seren, Tyus, what are you doing in here this time of night? Come back to bed.' Are you alright?'

I nodded. How could I explain what had happened? She led us back to bed, Seren clutching her doll in her arms when there was a loud knock on the front door.

'Who could be calling this time of night? Said Mum anxiously. 'They'll will have to call another time. I'm not answering it.'

The knocking continued accompanied by a well - known voice.

'Loria, it's me. Open the door!'

Mum didn't hesitate, 'Stefan, is it really you?'

She unlocked the door and there was Dad, standing as we all remembered him.

Loria, Tyus, Seren, I'm home.' said Dad gathering us all to him.

'Where have you been?' Mum asked through tears of happiness.

'It's a long story but I'll never go away again, I promise you.'

ACKNOWLEDGEMENT

Special thanks to Paul Halligan for proof reading and editing, supplying endless encouragement and tea.

ABOUT THE AUTHOR

Brenda Larkin

Brenda Larkin is a children's author living in Liverpool, U.K. She has always loved writing and telling stories to her children and her grandchildren. She has been a teacher and tutor for many years and has a passion for local history. The idea that history is beneath our feet or written on our street names has always fascinated her. She likes to explore this through her exciting mystery stories when modern day children travel to the past and have an adventure there.

The first book in the series is inspired by the medieval history of West Derby, Liverpool combined with a dramatic fantasy rescue quest.

Twitter @BrendaLarkinBooks
Instagram BrendaLarkinBooks

Printed in Poland
by Amazon Fulfillment
Poland Sp. z o.o., Wrocław

61166829R00052